Little Learning®

This Book Belongs To

Frances Trafelet

GLORIA ESTEFAN
The Magically Mysterious Adventures of
Noelle the Bulldog

illustrated by MICHAEL GARLAND

rayo

An Imprint of HarperCollinsPublishers

Noelle peeked through the gates at her wondrous new world,
with her Christmassy name and her own little girl.
She wasn't that pretty, quite far from the best,
with her brown brindle body and white-spotted chest.
With most of her features so oddly arranged,
compared to most Bulldogs she looked a bit strange.
"Welcome home," said the girl, as she patted her head.
"Would you like me to show you around your new spread?"

Then five spotted Dalmatians, their legs long and lean,
came bounding together like a well-oiled machine.
Each one of them sniffed her and asked her to play.
But then one barked, "You're different! Were you born far away?"
"I flew in a plane over mountains and seas,
like a bird flying over the tops of the trees."
They barked, "To the fish pond! We'll race you, young pup!"
Noelle tried to follow but couldn't catch up.

My legs are too short, thought Noelle, disappointed.
If these dogs have a club, there's no way I can join it.

She sat by the pond as her eyes lost their twinkle.
When suddenly up from below came a sprinkle.
Then hundreds of fish—shiny, colorful, bright—
swam up to the surface in joyous delight.

"You must be the new doggie! Come with us and play!
Let's go for a swim. We swim here all day!"

So Noelle dove right in but then sank like a rock.
The fish were all staring, their eyes wide with shock.

Then they swam close together and, lifting her high,
put her back on dry land and at once they all cried,
"We thought everyone everywhere knew how to swim."
"So did I," said Noelle. "That's why I jumped in!"

As she shook herself dry from her head to her toes,
a firefly perched on the tip of her nose.
"What are *you*?" asked Noelle, sensing she was in danger.
Was she going to be stung by this fuzzy, winged stranger?

"I'm sorry, Noelle, if I gave you a fright,
but what looks like a stinger is really a light.
We all have a gift," the small firefly chattered.
"I can light up the night, and my size doesn't matter."

Said Noelle, "But my coat and my color's not shiny or bright.
I might feel I belonged if, like you, I could light."

Then from eighteen feet high, swaying, tall as a tower,
came the powerful voice of a giant sunflower.
"You're quite special, Noelle, with a look you can't beat.
Dark and rich like the earth and, like chocolate, so sweet."

In the tallest of trees, branches scraping the sky,
dressed in feathery glory, birds were perched way up high.
They were squeaking and squawking with hardly a care.
Noelle yelled, "Can we talk?" They took off in the air.

"I'm a failure!" she cried. "Can't do anything right!
I can't talk to the birds, and my tail just won't light.
I can't swim, can't run fast, don't have shimmery colors.
I'm afraid I will never fit in with the others!"

Noelle sat on a stump as the sun said good-bye
and the moon said hello in the starry night sky.
Then the firefly spoke as her tail brightly beamed,
"You know, things are not always as bad as they seem.
In the day I am only one more flying creature,
but at night you can see my distinguishing feature.
Perhaps things are not what you might have expected,
but soon you will see we're all somehow connected."

And just when Noelle thought she couldn't get sadder,
the little girl came to see *what* was the matter.
"It's bedtime," she said. "Did you have a good day?"
Then she picked her up, kissed her, and swept her away.
In the little girl's arms, in a little brown heap,
curled up comfy and cozy, Noelle fell asleep.
And deep in her slumber she dreamed of the day
she'd find her mysterious, magical way.

Snuggled warm in her bed, waking up was quite hard,
but Noelle heard commotion outside in the yard.
The Dalmatians were flustered, quite clearly upset.
Noelle asked, "What's happened? Can't be that bad, I'll bet."
"We were tossing our ball, and it went way too far!"
They said, "Now we're afraid it's rolled under the car!
Our legs are so long there's no way we can fit.
Since we can't get the ball, there's no choice but to quit."

"Don't do that!" said Noelle. "I will get you the ball.
I can crawl under there with no trouble at all!"
With her short, chunky legs, young Noelle saved the day.
Then they made up a game *all* the doggies could play.

Noelle was so happy she'd gotten her wish,
she wanted to share her good news with the fish.
But the closer she got, the much louder she heard,
that the fish were all chanting one deafening word.
"HELP, HELP, HELP!" cried the fish, as Noelle saw with dread
how a fish out of water flopped around on his head.
"We were jumping for sport," the fish started to shout.
"He was jumping so high, by mistake he jumped out."

Noelle sprang into action; she knew what to do!
Put the fish in her mouth, but make sure not to chew.
So she carried him gently and dropped him back in.
And Noelle, in that moment, discovered her grin.

The fish said, "Noelle, you're a dog like no other!
If it wasn't for you, we'd have lost our dear brother!"
The firefly circled Noelle as he cheered,
"I knew you could do it, if you persevered!
But hurry, Noelle, someone else needs your skill.
The birds are so hungry they might soon fall ill!"
So Noelle to the kitchen ran off without warning,
to get what she'd seen in the pantry that morning.

She fashioned a stairway with cans of baked beans,
sacks of flour and rice, and a case of sardines.
She pushed and she stacked with her strong little snout.
She climbed and she climbed. Her legs almost gave out!
But she snatched the seed bag with her little front teeth,
dragged it out to the birds, who awaited their feast,
and then ripped it wide open and said, "By the way,
I'll make sure that I get you some seeds every day!"

"Well, well, well," said the birds, now completely impressed.
"You don't cease to amaze us, Noelle! You're the *best*!"
Everyone gathered around, she was showered with praise,
and they sang of her magical, mystical ways.
Noelle just lit up. She was bursting with pride.
Her strength and true beauty had come from inside.
And though viewed from the outside you couldn't quite tell,
there was never a dog like the dog named Noelle!

For Nayib and Emily

CD CREDITS:
Noelle's Song (Been Wishin') 3:40
Performed by: Gloria Estefan
Words and Music by: Gloria M. Estefan
Produced by: Emilio Estefan, Gaitan Bros. for Crescent Moon, Inc.
Arranged by: Gaitan Bros.
Acoustic and Electric Guitars: Marco Linares; Percussion: Archie Peña;
Recording Engineers: Alfred Figueroa, Gaitan Bros.;
Vocal Engineer: Sebastian Krys, Gaitan Bros.; Mixing Engineer: Alfred Figueroa;
Assistant Engineer: Ryan Wolff; Recorded and Mixed at: Crescent Moon Studios,
Miami, FL; Published by: Foreign Imported Productions & Publishing, Inc. (BMI)
© 2005 Estefan Enterprises, Inc./ ℗ 2005 Sony BMG Music Entertainment, Inc.
Manufactured by HarperCollins Publishers, 10 East 53rd Street, New York, NY 10022.
WARNING: All rights reserved. Unauthorized duplication
is a violation of applicable laws.

THE MAGICALLY MYSTERIOUS ADVENTURES OF NOELLE THE BULLDOG. Copyright © 2005 by Estefan
Enterprises, Inc. All rights reserved. Printed in the United States of America. No part
of this book may be used or reproduced in any manner whatsoever without written
permission except in the case of brief quotations embodied in critical articles and
reviews. For information address HarperCollins Publishers Inc., 10 East 53rd Street,
New York, NY 10022.
HarperCollins books may be purchased for educational, business, or sales promotional
use. For information please write: Special Markets Department, HarperCollins
Publishers Inc., 10 East 53rd Street, New York, NY 10022.
First Rayo edition published 2005.
Library of Congress Cataloging-in-Publication Data is available.
ISBN 0-06-082623-1 (English) — ISBN 0-06-082626-6 (Spanish)
05 06 07 08 09 RRD 10 9 8 7 6 5 4 3 2 1